Sally's Snowman

Story by Annette Smith

Illustrations by Meredith Thomas

Rigby®

A Harcourt Achieve Imprint

www.Rigby.com
1-800-531-5015

Sally is looking at the snow.

Here comes Sally.

"Look, Mom," said Sally.

"Here is a little snowman."

The sun is on

the little snowman.

"Mom! Mom!" said Sally.

"**Look** at my little snowman."

Mom is looking at

Sally's snowman.

"Come here, Sally," said Mom.

"Here is a big snowball."

"Look at the **big** snowman,"

said Sally.